Robin Boyden

GERALD
Needs a Friend

Frances Lincoln
Children's Books

Gerald's garden
was his whole world.

He had everything
he needed.

He spent most of his days
watering the plants

and picking fruit and vegetables.

With them he made jams
and pickles so he could taste
the summer garden even
in the winter.

Every evening, Gerald had tea at 5 o'clock, sharp. Then he made a camomile tea.

He read twenty pages of his book, brushed his teeth and was in bed by 7 o'clock on-the-dot.

One morning, as usual, Gerald woke up early.

He put on his clothes...

brushed his fur,

collected his grocery bags,

and headed into town.

But today was unusual.
There was a new stall in the market
run by two excitable mice.

The whole town seemed to be gathered around.
Gerald felt flustered near all the busy people.

Gerald watched in awe as the two mice found...

a new button for
hedgehog's coat,

a way for a young duckling to fly,

and a scooter for little
turtle who dreamed of going fast!

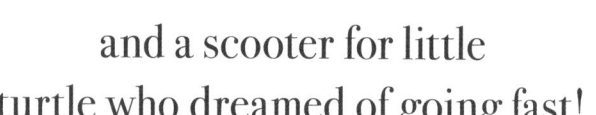

Soon, Gerald was the only one left
in front of the mice's stall.

"Hello sir, my name is Marcy."

"And I'm Marcel. What do you want more than anything?"

"Nothing! I have everything I need," Gerald squeaked.

"Well there's always room for more fun!"

"Perhaps you'd like a new hobby?" said Marcy.

"Or to learn a musical instrument?" said Marcel.

"Or a new look?"
they sang.

The costumes made
Gerald feel shy,

then **funny**,

then **cheerful**,

then **confident**...

and brave

and fantastic!

Gerald was a pirate captain, riding the high seas
with First Mate Marcy and Deck Hand Marcel.

They searched for treasure, followed ancient
maps and dodged fearsome rivals but just
as they were about to encounter a pirate
crew of stuffed toys...

The town clock struck 5.

The cuckoo clock in the market struck 5.

All the clocks in town struck 5.

"Oh no! I'm late, I'm late!"
Gerald cried. "I always have
tea at 5 o'clock, sharp!"

When he got home
he had dinner
in a rush,

so he would have
time to make
camomile
tea,

before he read twenty
pages of his book,

then brushed
his teeth in
time to be...

in bed by 7 o'clock, on-the-dot.

But for the first time in his life, he couldn't sleep.

In the morning he went to pick some fruit for breakfast, but he wasn't hungry.

Nothing he did felt like it normally did. He had a funny flat feeling.

But luckily, Gerald knew how to make himself feel cheerful.

He gave Marcy and Marcel a
picnic box carefully packed
with all of his beautiful
jams and pickles.

"These are for you to say
thank you. For the most
fun I've ever had."

"Gerald this is **delicious!**"

"I've made plenty. In fact, there's enough for
everybody at my house!"

The friends played and laughed all day and night.

Gerald realised having
everything he needed was
no fun without friends to
share it with.

For Max, River, and Willow
– R.B.

Text and illustration © 2021 Robin Boyden.

First published in 2021 by Frances Lincoln Children's Books, an imprint of The Quarto Group.

100 Cummings Center, Suite 265D, Beverly, MA 01915, USA.

T +1 978-282-9590 F +1 078-283-2742 www.QuartoKnows.com

The right of Robin Boyden to be identified as the author and illustrator of this work has been asserted by them in accordance with the Copyright,

Designs and Patents Act, 1988 (United Kingdom).

A catalogue record for this book is available from the British Library.

ISBN 978-0-7112-5208-0

The illustrations were created digitally

Set in Bodoni 72

Published by Katie Cotton

Edited by Lucy Brownridge

Designed by Zoë Tucker

Production by Dawn Cameron

Printed in Guangdong, China CC022022

9 8 7 6 5 4 3 2 1

MIX
Paper from
responsible sources
FSC® C008047
FSC
www.fsc.org